Sir Galahad
and the
Grail

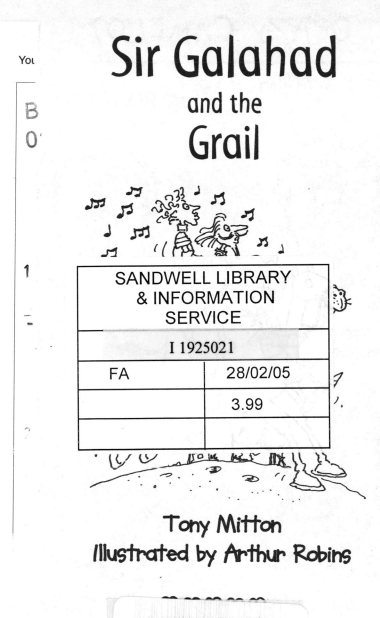

Tony Mitton
Illustrated by Arthur Robins

CRAZY CAMELOT

MEET THE KNIGHTS OF THE ROUND TABLE:

King Arthur
with his sword so bright,

Sir Percival,
a wily knight.

Sir Kay,
a chap whose hopes are high,

Sir Lancelot,
makes ladies sigh.

Sir Gawain,
feeling rather green,

Sir Galahad,
so young and keen.

Sir Ack,
who's fond of eating lots,

Sir Mordred,
hatching horrid plots.

Morgana,
Arthur's wicked
sister,

Merlin.
That's me,
your wizard mister!

To Sir Neil
& the Lady Christine, from Tony Mitton,
scribe to Merlin

To Sir Hayden Thomas Skerry,
from Arthur Robins

ORCHARD BOOKS
96 Leonard Street, London EC2A 4XD
Orchard Books Australia
32/45-51 Huntley Street, Alexandria, NSW 2015
First published in Great Britain in 2004
First paperback edition 2004
Text © Tony Mitton 2004
Illustrations © Arthur Robins 2004
The rights of Tony Mitton to be identified as the author
and Arthur Robins as the illustrator of this work
have been asserted by them in accordance with the
Copyright, Designs, and Patents Act, 1988.
A CIP catalogue record for this book is available
from the British Library.
ISBN 1 84121 474 4 (hardback)
ISBN 1 84362 001 4 (paperback)
1 3 5 7 9 10 8 6 4 2 (hardback)
1 3 5 7 9 10 8 6 4 2 (paperback)
Printed in Great Britain

In the days of good King Arthur
when knights wore suits of metal,
they rode around with a clanking sound
like the clatter of pot on kettle.

'Cos if you're dressed for combat,
with a thick tin can for a jacket,
you only have to scratch your nose
and it makes a right old racket.

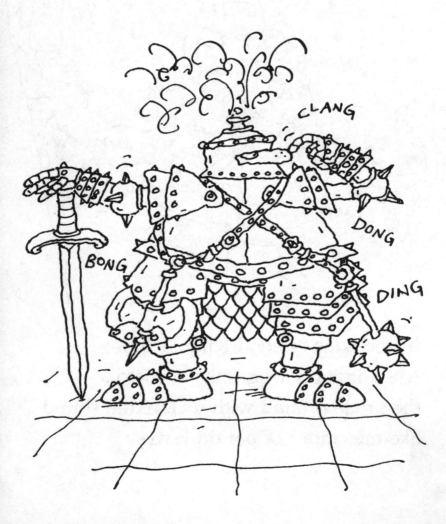

I am the wizard Merlin.
I've seen and heard it all.
See how the stories softly swirl
inside my crystal ball.

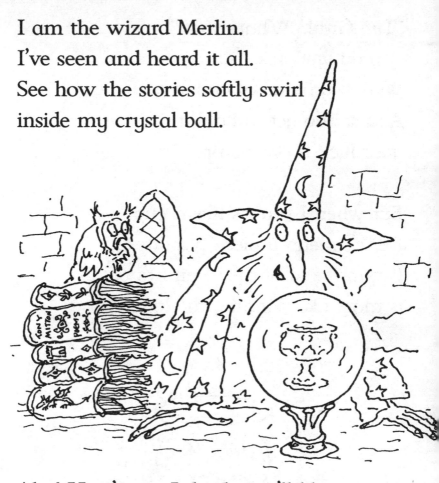

Aha! Here's one I think you'll like.
I'm sure it cannot fail.
It tells how great Sir Galahad
set out to get the Grail.

"The Grail? What's that?" you
    may well ask.
Well, it's a kind of cup.
And if you get to hold it,
your luck is on the up.

But when I say it's like a cup
I don't mean a piece of pottery.
Getting hold of the Grail (it's gold!)
is more like winning the lottery.

This Holy Grail was far away,
lost to a foreign land,
locked up as a precious treasure
by a greedy robber band.

A legend told that the three best knights
would one day cross the sea
and bring the Grail back home to show
to folks like you and me.

But here's the hitch: In Camelot,
the Best Knight wasn't there,
for at the Great Round Table
there stood…the Empty Chair.

Upon the chair some words were carved
and this is what they said:
If you're not the best, don't try the test.
Sit here, and you'll be dead.

So the chair just stood there empty
as no one seemed to fit.
"Ah, well," sighed good King Arthur,
"we'll have to wait a bit."

We can't send the three best knights
    out there,
if the Best Knight's not yet come.
And sending two just wouldn't do.
That would be simply dumb!

Now, one day brave Sir Lancelot
was riding through the wood,
when he saw a glow of golden light
and it made him feel so good.

And the glow became a vision
of the Grail, so bright and fine
that he span around and fell to
    the ground,
as if he'd had too much wine.

The nuns of a nearby convent
found him and put him to bed.
They gave him a funny potion
which helped to clear his head.

Then they brought him a lad
    with golden hair
who looked both brave and true.
And they said, "When you go
    to Camelot,
please take this boy with you.

"He was left with us as a baby,
but he's growing big and strong.
We can't keep a man in a convent.
That would be really wrong."

"Yes, teach me to be a knight like you," said the eager, youthful lad.

Teach me to fight and do what's right. My name is Galahad.

So Lancelot took that keen, young man
and taught him the tricks of the trade:
how to stay on a horse and, yes,
   of course,
how to wield a big, strong blade.

How to put on a helmet the right
    way round,
and fasten an iron boot.
How not to fall down like a circus clown
when wearing a two-ton suit.

Galahad learned so quickly,
he could gallop before he could trot.
So, soon it was time to introduce
the lad to Camelot.

"My friends," cried bold Sir Lancelot,
"look at this lovely sight.
See what I found in the forest:
a brand new, noble knight!"

Galahad nodded a greeting,
then sat in the Empty Chair...
Everyone shrieked and pointed,
"Be careful! Don't sit there...!"

"Why not?" said golden Galahad.

It seems to fit just fine.
Besides, I feel it in my bones:
this chair is clearly mine.

King Arthur leaped and punched the air,
"Whoopee! He's come. At last!
This lad must be our true Best Knight.
Our long, long wait is past."

He got young Galahad to kneel
and knighted him at his feet.
"Arise, Sir Galahad," he said,
"and take your rightful seat.

"Our company's complete," he cried.
"At last our Best Knight's here!
Let's send out for a takeaway
and Camelot's best beer."

Just as the meal was ending,
Sir Lancelot spoke up.
"I saw a vision the other day
of the missing Golden Cup."

Everyone gasped in wonder.
"The Cup! The Holy Grail!
That means it's time to bring it home.
Come on. Let's hit the trail!"

"Ah, no," cut in wise Merlin.
"This is a special quest.
It's meant for three, and they must be
tip-top - the very best!"

Galahad will be Number One.
At fighting Lancelot's ace.
Now who's got good survival skills
to fill the final place...?

Everyone looked at Percival,
the wild knight from the West.
"That's it!" said Merlin, nodding.
"These three knights make the best."

So Galahad and Lancelot
and Percival agreed
that they would ride both far and wide
until they'd done the deed.

But where the Holy Grail was,
they hardly had a notion.
They only knew it lay out there
across the foaming ocean.

"I had a dream," said Galahad,
"that it was somewhere hot."
So off they sailed with suntan cream
from chilly Camelot.

They came to a far off country
with lots of sun and sand.
And they went ashore, saying,
   "Let's explore.
This seems a likely land."

But no one knew of the Golden Grail,
when they tried to ask the way.
And the three knights plodded
   staunchly on,
day after weary day.

They encountered many adventures,
being so bold and brave.
For they visited towns and castles
and stopped to check each cave.

They met with giants and dragons
and serpents with many heads.
They grappled with trolls and demons,
found scorpions in their beds.

And the sand got into their sandwiches
and tickled between their toes,
while midges bit them on the ear
and got right up their nose.

But though they fought with many a foe
in battles fierce and bold,
they never heard a whisper
of the Grail that glowed so gold.

Till one day Galahad woke up
with both blue eyes agleam.
"Surprise, surprise! I've got it, guys!
I've seen it in a dream."

The Grail's in a ruined fortress,
out in the desert sands.
No one goes there nowadays,
except for robber bands.

So off they went, that trusty trio,
across the desert dunes.
To blow away their boredom,
they whistled silly tunes.

Till there it stood, with broken walls
and towers all tumbled down.
"Be careful now," said Lancelot,
and gave a wary frown.

For, as he guessed, inside the fort
was hidden many a guard.
And all of them had cutlasses,
and all of them were hard.

So, though our knights were weary,
they battled: *Biff! Baff! Boff!*
They made those robbers leap about
and sent them howling off.

They searched the ruined fortress
and found a secret stair.
They stopped to light a candle,
then tiptoed down with care.

"This could be it," said Galahad.
"There's something here, no doubt."
A chilly draught came wafting through
and blew their candle out.

They shuffled slowly forwards
towards a distant glow.
It shone both bright and golden.
Galahad cried, "O-ho!"

He jumped around, delighted,
and pointed at the gleam.
"Look, Perce and Lance, I want to dance!
It's just like in my dream!"

I knew we'd get to do it.
I knew we wouldn't fail.
It's standing right in front of us:
the shining Holy Grail.

But Lancelot and Percival
were dazzled by its glow.
So Galahad got hold of it
and cried,

And go they did. They mounted up
and went off at a trot,
then after many weeks returned
to castle Camelot.

You'd think they'd won the football
to see folk jump and shout.
King Arthur called a holiday
and everyone came out.

And then he threw a special feast
to celebrate the Cup.
"Come on, young Galahad," he cried.
"Please, hold the trophy up!"

But as he did, the dining hall
was filled with golden light,
and nobody could look at it,
except the true Best Knight.

Then, as the dazzle faded,
they opened up their eyes,
and *wow!* the Grail and Galahad
were heading for the skies...

A magic voice came booming down,
"They're much too good for you.
Sir Galahad will guard the Grail
in Heaven, out of view."

"Well, never mind," King Arthur shrugged.

I still say that we've done it. Before it floated up to Heaven the Cup was ours. We won it!

So, there's the tale of how the Grail
came back to Camelot.
And this is Merlin checking out
and winding up the plot.

And now, to take my exit,
I'll make myself glow bright...
till soon I'm just a golden haze -
and then I'm out of sight...

OOOOOOH!

CRAZY CAMELOT CAPERS

Written by Tony Mitton
Illustrated by Arthur Robins

Crazy Camelot Capers are available from all good bookshops,
or can be ordered direct from the publisher:
Orchard Books, PO BOX 29, Douglas IM99 1BQ
Credit card orders please telephone 01624 836000
or fax 01624 837033
or e-mail: bookshop@enterprise.net for details.

To order please quote title, author and ISBN
and your full name and address.
Cheques and postal orders should be
made payable to 'Bookpost plc'.
Postage and packing is FREE within the UK
(overseas customers should add £1.00 per book).

Prices and availability are subject to change.